E612.8 GEL

Gelman
BODY DE
0590470

D0565267

2005

BODY DETECTIVES

A Book About the Five Senses

by Rita Golden Gelman

illustrated by Elroy Freem

SCHOLASTIC INC.
New York   Toronto   London   Auckland   Sydney

Ta daaaaa!

Presenting the true story of the
  smelly
  feely
  ear-drumming
  sight-seeing
  taste-tingling
  team of
    BODY DETECTIVES,
    otherwise known as
    THE FIVE SENSES.

DRIFTWOOD PUBLIC LIBRARY
801 SW HWY 101
LINCOLN CITY, OREGON 97367

No part of this publication may be reproduced in whole or in part,
or stored in a retrieval system, or transmitted in any form
or by any means, electronic, mechanical, photocopying, recording,
or otherwise, without written permission of the publisher.
For information regarding permission, write to Scholastic Inc.,
555 Broadway, New York, NY 10012.

ISBN 0-590-47019-1

Text copyright © 1994 by Rita Golden Gelman.
Illustrations copyright © 1994 by Mark Teague.
All rights reserved. Published by Scholastic Inc.

12 11 10 9 8 7 6 5 4 3 2 1   4 5 6 7 8 9/9

Printed in the U.S.A.   08

First Scholastic printing, September 1994

Dedicated with love and thanks
    to taste buds and smell receptors.
Without them, hot fudge would taste the same as oatmeal.

Your brain is the big boss.
   It's the head.
   It's the chief.
   It's the captain of your body.
Everything you feel or say or do is directed by your brain.
   It's a
      super-sensational,
      what-a-creational,
      brilliant
      and trustworthy
      brain.

But your brain is all snuggled up in your head, hiding inside a hard and bony skull. In order to know what's going on in the outside world, your brain needs help.

Enter please:

THE FIVE SENSES, your body's detectives.

Your senses are made up of billions
of microscopic nerve cells called

SENSE RECEPTORS.

All sense receptors are detectives.
Their job is to find out about the world.
   They gather evidence,
   uncover the truth,
   collect the facts,
   and send all the information to the brain.
The information travels along tiny roads called nerves.

Everything you know starts out in your sense receptors, travels along the nerves, and ends up in your brain.

So get the bands to play the music.
Let the banners be unfurled.
Shout the praises
of the number-one detectives in the world:

THE SENSE RECEPTORS.

Sense Number One: SIGHT

Sight receptors do the seeing.
There are two kinds: the cones and the rods.

CONE   ROD

The cones detect color. They work the day shift...

and at night, if there's light. But when it's dark, the cones are
off duty,
finished,
done with their day.
The rods work in the dark, but they can't detect colors.
All they see are shades of gray. That's why we can't see
colors in the dark.

Light rays are reflected off the dog.
They pass through the cornea and the lens of your eye.
When they get to the retina, they bump into the rods and cones.

Whoosh! The rods and cones turn the light rays into
nerve impulses. The information races along the sight nerves
until it gets to the brain.

"Well, well," says the brain when it gets the message.
"That looks like a dog."

Sense Number Two: HEARING

Sound receptors do the hearing.
They hang out in your ears,
but not on those flaps on the sides of your head.
The flaps are only one part of the complicated machine
we call an ear.

The noise of an airplane creates sound waves in the air.
The flaps catch the sound waves and pass them through
the tunnels. At the end of each tunnel, the sound waves
bump into a little circle of skin called an eardrum.

When the sound waves hit the drum, it shakes.
   Then the drum shakes the hammer.
   And the hammer shakes the anvil.
   And the anvil shakes the stirrup.
   And the stirrup . . . at last . . . shakes some tiny hairs inside
      the bone-that-looks-like-a-snail.
The hairs are a part of your sound receptors.

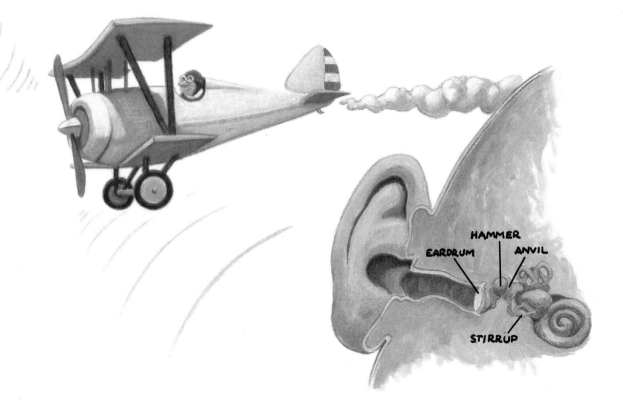

Whoosh! The sound receptors turn the sound waves into nerve impulses. The message races along the hearing nerves until it gets to the brain.

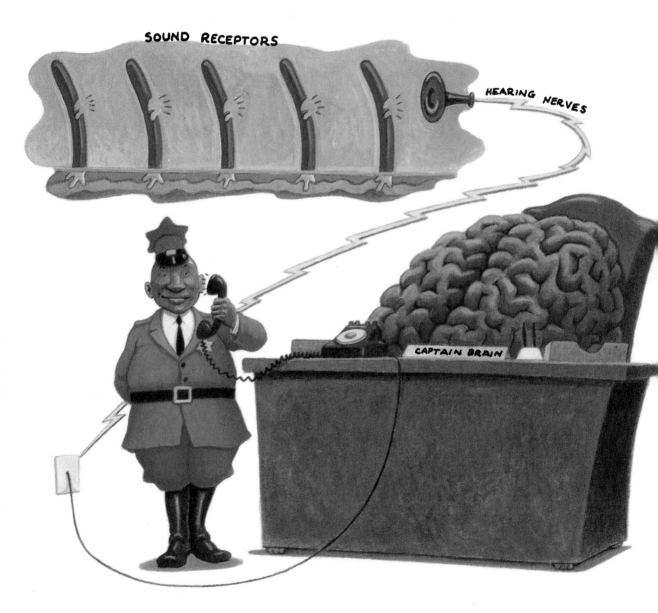

"Well, well," says the brain. "That sounds like a plane."

Sound waves vibrate.
Eardrums wiggle.
Hammers, anvils, stirrups jiggle.
Detectives in your inner ear
Inform the brain.
That's when you hear.

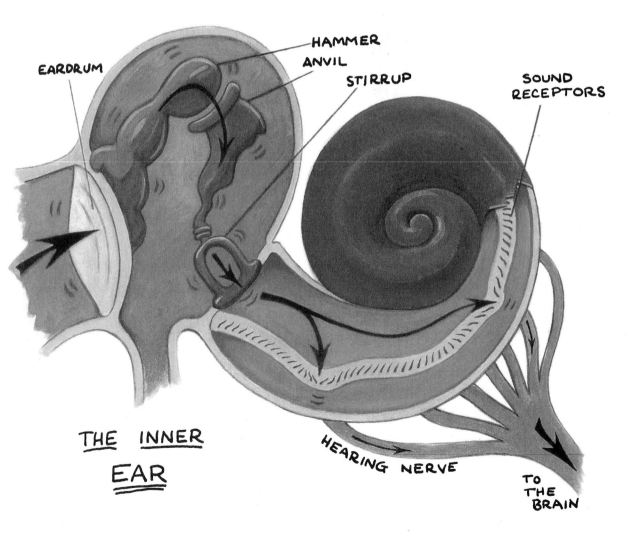

EARDRUM

HAMMER
ANVIL
STIRRUP

SOUND
RECEPTORS

THE INNER
EAR

HEARING NERVE

TO
THE
BRAIN

Sense Number Three: SMELL

Smell receptors investigate tiny smelly things that float in the air.
That's what smells are, chemical substances that you can't see.
Your smell receptors hang out way at the top of your nose,
in between your eyes. There are about ten million of them.

Each receptor has about 150 hairs, called cilia, sticking out
from one end. . .and nerves coming out of the other.
The cilia react to those floating things, those chemicals in the air.

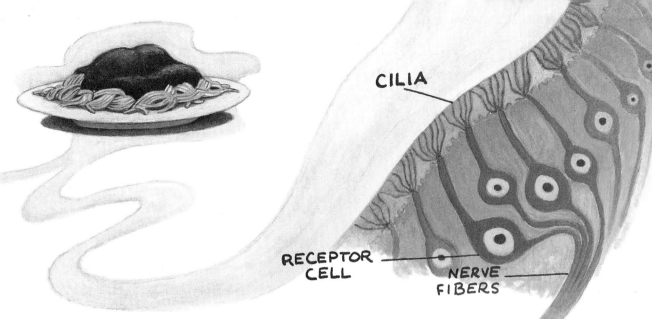

CILIA

RECEPTOR
CELL

NERVE
FIBERS

Whoosh! The smell receptors turn the chemical information into nerve impulses and send the message racing to the brain.

"Well, well," says the brain. "That smells like spaghetti."

Sense Number Four: TASTE

Taste buds are little bumps on your tongue.
They detect chemicals in your food and drink.

Each bud is a team of about fifty taste receptors.
In the middle of each bud is a tiny hole called a pore.
When food is dissolved in your saliva, it seeps into the pores.
That's when it bumps into the taste receptors.

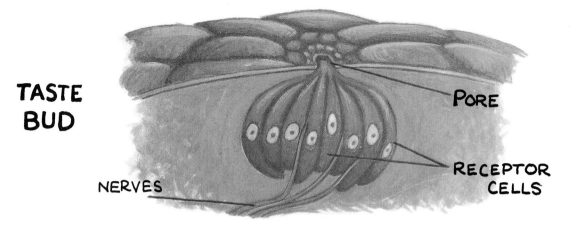

TASTE BUD

NERVES

PORE

RECEPTOR CELLS

Whoosh! The taste receptors turn the chemical information into nerve impulses and send it racing to the brain.

"Well, well," says the brain. "That tastes like ice cream."

If your tongue is dry, and the food is dry,
your taste buds don't taste.
Only liquids can enter the holes in your taste buds.

It's a little bit weird,
But it really is true.
Taste buds are clever,
But limited, too.
They only taste sour
And bitter
And sweet
And salty.
That's all that they taste
When we eat.
All other flavors,
We "taste" with our nose.
It's hard to believe,
But that's how it goes.

Most tastes are really smells.
And that's why you can't taste much
when your nose is stuffed.

DRIFTWOOD
801 SW
LINCOLN CITY, OREGON 97367

Sense Number Five: TOUCH

Touch receptors are in your skin. Because of them, you know when something is touching you.

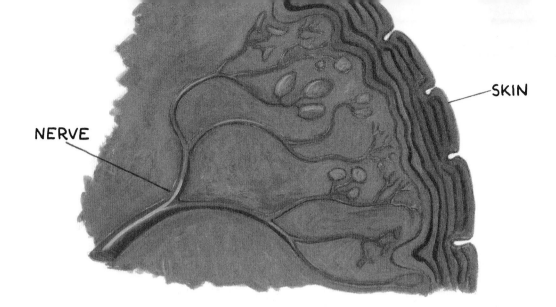

NERVE

SKIN

You feel a hot iron and pull your hand away.
You feel sandpaper and know that it's rough.
Even a gentle touch sends a nerve impulse to your brain.

"Aaah," says the brain. "That feels good."

CAPTAIN BRAIN

Thank goodness for
receptors
and detectives
and the rest.
Without 'em, we'd be lima beans or cantaloupes at best.

HEADQUARTERS OF THE BODY DETECTIVES

CAPTAIN BRAIN

SMELL RECEP

TASTE

So let's hear it for eyes
And noses and tongues
And fingers and hammers vibrational.
Without 'em we're nothing,
Nothing at all.
And with 'em, we're super-sensational!

A Poem About the Senses

We have five senses:
   seeing, touching, hearing, tasting, smelling.
They tell us about the world.

We see with our eyes.
We see color and size.
We see purple and yellow and white.
We know about big and little and long
Because of our sense of sight.

We know there are smiles
And shadows
And shapes.
We can tell the night from the day.
We know there are rainbows and shooting stars —
We see them from far away.

But our eyes don't know
About hot or cold
Or the slimy skin of an eel.
For *those* we need the sense of touch.
For *those* we have to feel.

We feel a kiss.
We feel a pin.
Our sense of touch is in our skin.
We feel a sting,
An itch,
A pain.
The cold of snow,
The wet of rain.

We feel *smooth*.
We feel *sharp*.
But we cannot *feel*
The song of a harp.
We have to *hear* a lullaby,
The sound of wind,
A baby's cry.

A carousel,
A quiet hum.
Rain on the roof,
The bang of a drum.

Laughter,
Songs,
And football cheers.
Our sense of hearing is in our ears.

But we cannot hear
The taste of grapes
Or spaghetti
Or blueberry pies.
Tasting happens inside our mouths
And not in our ears or our eyes.

Lemons are sour.
They're hard to eat.
Pickles are salty
And sugar is sweet.
Vinegar isn't the same as tea.
My taste buds know
And they tell me.

But we cannot taste
Or hear
Or feel
Or see the smell of a rose,
Or a skunk
Or smoke
Or soap.
Our sense of smell is in our nose.

We smell the ocean,
Roasting meat.
Candles burning,
People's feet.

Cheeses smell.
Puppies, too.
Sometimes, even babies do.

Our senses work together.
They're sort of like a team.
We see and feel and smell a flower.
We see and feel and hear a stream.

We see and feel and taste our food.
And some of it, we smell.
And when we take a bite and chew,
We *hear* our food as well.

Because of all our senses,
The world is very real.
How nice it is
    to see
    and hear
    and taste
    and smell
    and feel.